DATE			

Ann Schweninger

Christmas Secrets

·FATHER· ·BUTTERCUP. ·BUTTON BROWN· ·MOTHER· ·DAISY·

Viking Kestrel

First Edition
Copyright © 1984 by Ann Schweninger
All rights reserved

Viking Kestrel
First published in 1984 by Viking Kestrel Books
40 West 23rd Street, New York, New York 10010

Published by Penguin Books Ltd. in U.K.
Harmondsworth, Middlesex, England

Published simultaneously in Canada by Penguin Books Canada Limited
Printed in Japan.
1   2   3   4   5   88   87   86   85   84

Library of Congress Cataloging in Publication Data
Schweninger, Ann.   Christmas secrets.
Summary: The Rabbit children's Christmas preparations include building
a mystery snowman, writing letters to Santa, and baking Christmas cookies.
[1. Christmas—Fiction.   2. Rabbits—Fiction]   I. Title.
PZ7.S41263Ch   1984   [E]   83-16983
ISBN 0-670-22109-0

For Ron

The Snowman

The Letter

Christmas Eve

NOW LET'S MAKE THREE SPECIAL ONES.

LET'S TAKE SOME OUT TO THE CAROLERS.

BUT NOT THE SPECIAL ONES!